TRANSPORTATION TECHNOLOGY

INSPIRED BY NATURE

by Wendy Hinote Lanier

FOCUS READERS

FOCUS READERS

WWW.FOCUSREADERS.COM

Focus Readers is distributed by North Star Editions:
sales@northstareditions.com | 888-417-0195

Produced for Focus Readers by Red Line Editorial.

Content Consultant: Ximin He, PhD, Assistant Professor of Materials Science and Engineering, University of California, Los Angeles

Photographs ©: hxdbzxy/Shutterstock Images, cover, 1; Loic Lagarde/Moment Mobile/Getty Images, 4–5; mauribo/iStockphoto, 7; ajansen/iStockphoto, 9; FloridaStock/Shutterstock Images, 10–11; Skycolors/Shutterstock Images, 13; wwing/iStockphoto, 15; Kenneth Cheung/NASA, 17; Willyam Bradberry/Shutterstock Images, 18–19; Red Line Editorial, 20; katoosha/iStockphoto, 23; Steve Gschmeissner/Science Source, 24–25; Airbus Xinhua News Agency/Newscom, 27; chombosan/iStockphoto, 28

ISBN
978-1-63517-944-6 (hardcover)
978-1-64185-046-9 (paperback)
978-1-64185-248-7 (ebook pdf)
978-1-64185-147-3 (hosted ebook)

Library of Congress Control Number: 2018932009

Printed in the United States of America
Mankato, MN
May, 2018

ABOUT THE AUTHOR

Wendy Hinote Lanier is a native Texan and former elementary teacher who writes and speaks for children and adults on a variety of topics. She is the author of more than 30 books for children and young adults.

TABLE OF CONTENTS

14
15
500

CHAPTER 1

ON THE LAND

Before modern transportation existed, people lived most of their lives in one small area. Today, many people travel all over the world. But moving from one place to another can be difficult. Scientists are always looking for faster and safer methods of travel.

In Japan, bullet trains carry travelers as fast as 199 miles per hour (320 km/h).

Some of the best ideas for technology come from nature. Scientists have been inspired by nature for hundreds of years. They study nature to find ways to solve human problems. Then, they mimic nature's methods. This process is known as biomimicry.

An example of biomimicry is the redesigned bullet train in Japan. Earlier bullet trains had flat noses that pushed a wall of air ahead of them. This created booming noises as the train entered tunnels. The noises were so loud that they damaged tunnels.

Engineers found a solution to the problem by watching kingfisher birds.

The kingfisher uses its splash-less dive to sneak up on fish.

The kingfisher dives into water without making a splash. The bird's long, narrow beak makes this possible. A rounded beak would push water forward. But the kingfisher's beak is pointed. As the bird dives, water flows smoothly past its beak.

New bullet trains have a nose shaped like a kingfisher's beak. These trains are faster and quieter. They no longer create booming noises. Plus, they use up to 15 percent less energy.

Biomimicry has also led to many car designs. One example is the McLaren P1 car. This car was inspired by the sailfish. The sailfish is one of the fastest fish in the ocean. The force of water causes most fish to swim slower. But the sailfish's scales create small whirls of air. These pockets of air prevent water from touching the fish.

Designers created similar scales for the McLaren P1. They applied the scales

The McLaren P1 is a hybrid car. It has both a gasoline engine and an electric motor.

to the **ducts** leading to the engine. The P1 engine is extremely powerful. It needs large amounts of air to burn fuel. Air also cools the engine. The scale-lined ducts feed 17 percent more air into the engine. This increase in air makes the engine more **efficient**. Thanks to nature, cars can achieve more power using less energy.

CHAPTER 2

IN THE AIR

Scientists dreamed of flying long before airplanes were invented. They studied birds to invent the first airplanes. Today, birds continue to inspire new aircraft.

In the 1970s, an engineer wanted to make airplanes more efficient. He looked to eagles for inspiration. Eagles curl the tips of their wings upward as they fly.

An eagle in flight curls the tips of its wings.

This helps them gain height. The engineer designed a vertical wing tip for airplanes. The wing tip, called a winglet, works similarly to an eagle's. The winglet makes it easier for the plane to cut through air. It also creates **lift**. As a result, the plane requires less fuel. Using less fuel also

FLYING V

Large birds such as geese fly in the shape of a V. The birds in the front create whirling masses of air. The masses of air help lift the birds in the back. This allows the birds to use less energy. Military pilots use the same shape when flying in a group. This way, they use less fuel.

Planes with winglets tend to be quieter than planes without.

helps reduce air pollution. Today, most passenger planes have a form of winglets.

Aircraft often cause noise pollution. Noise pollution occurs when high levels of noise disturb human or animal life. Scientists want to make quieter airplanes. To learn how, they have looked to the owl.

Owls make very little noise when they fly. They have unique wings that reduce sound. Feathers at the front of the wing are shaped like a comb. As the owl flies, the edges of the feathers break up the flow of air. Feathers at the back of the wing have a **fringe**. This breaks up the air even more. The smaller masses of air create less noise. Owl feathers are also very soft. They absorb the sound made by the owl's wings.

Scientists hope to add similar designs to airplanes. They designed an aircraft propeller blade with a comb-like edge. The blade mimics an owl's front wing feathers. Owls have inspired other ideas,

The leading edge (left) of an owl feather has a comb-like pattern. The trailing edge (right) has a fringe.

too. One is a fringe that attaches to airplane wings. Another is a coating for the plane's landing gear. The coating would mimic the texture of owl feathers.

SHAPE-CHANGING WINGS

Birds can adjust the amount their feathers overlap. This changes the shapes of their wings. Birds use different wing shapes as they fly. For instance, they make their wings long when they turn. To fly faster, they make their wings short. A shorter wing helps reduce **drag**.

Scientists hope to use shape-changing wings on airplanes. They are designing a wing made of many parts. These tiny, lightweight parts can form different shapes as the plane flies. As a result, the wings can bend and twist. The parts are covered in strips of a flexible material. The strips mimic bird feathers. They move across one another as the wing changes shape. The strips create a smooth wing surface.

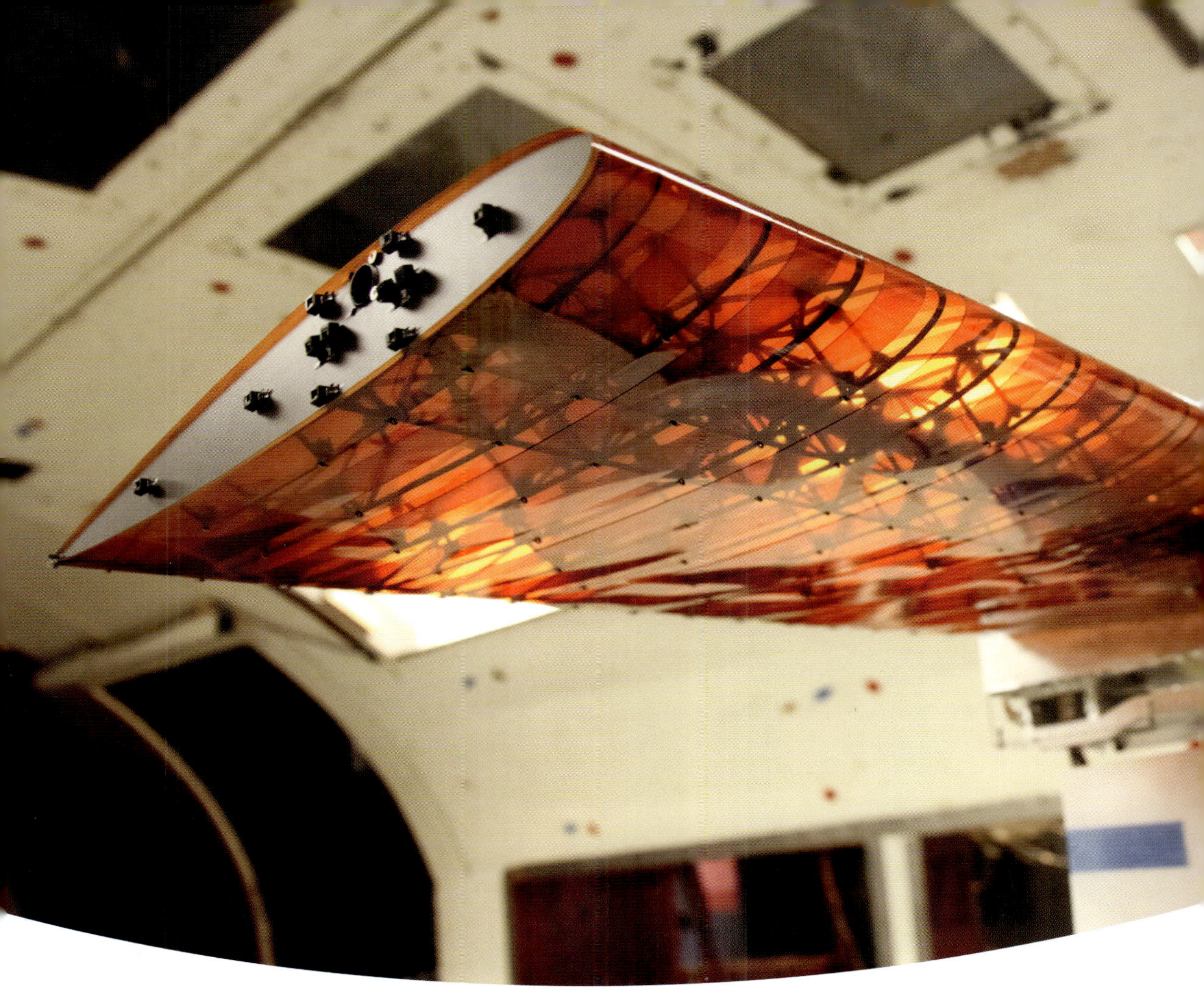

The shape-changing wing is less rigid than other wings.

Shape-changing wings allow planes to move more easily through the air. They are also lighter than other wings. Therefore, the plane uses less energy as it flies. This saves fuel.

CHAPTER 3

IN THE WATER

The way animals move through water has always fascinated scientists. Many scientists study sea animals to learn from their movements. This gives them ideas for new transportation technology.

Sharks are fast swimmers. Scientists studied sharkskin to find out why. The skin is lined with small, tooth-like scales.

Sharks swim in short bursts of speed.

These structures are called denticles. As a shark swims, the denticles direct water over the shark's body. This allows for swift, easy movement. It also keeps

SMOOTH SWIMMING

Without denticles, the shark would cause whirling masses of water.

Denticles direct the water smoothly over the shark's body.

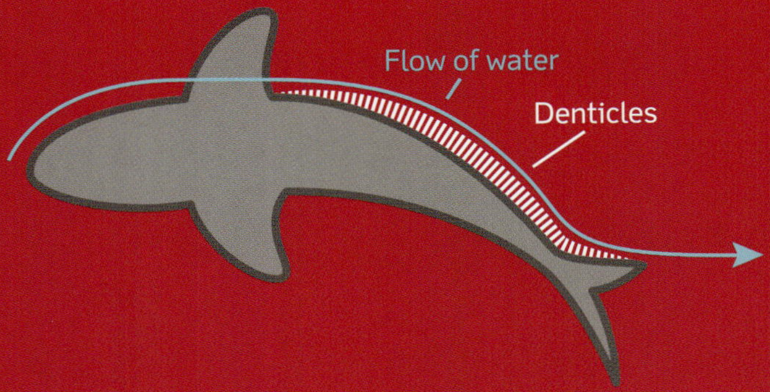

tiny sea creatures from attaching to the shark's body. Thanks to their denticles, sharks have few to no **parasites**.

Scientists made a material that mimics sharkskin. It uses the same pattern of small structures. The material can be used on boats and airplanes. It keeps algae from attaching to boats. It also reduces drag and saves energy. The material could be used on many surfaces to resist **bacteria**.

Octopuses have inspired scientists as well. These animals are skilled at escaping predators. An octopus swims headfirst away from danger. To swim, the octopus takes water into its body.

Then, it squirts the water out through a funnel. This is a tube-shaped organ near the octopus's head. The force of the water pushes the octopus forward. The octopus changes direction by turning the funnel.

Scientists have created a similar system for boats. Four balloon-like

A WHALE OF A SUB

Killer whales are one of the fastest animals in the ocean. One company sells a submarine inspired by killer whales. The submarine can take two people approximately 5 feet (1.5 m) underwater. It can move up to 50 miles per hour (81 km/h). It can even jump out of the water, similar to a whale. The submarine's fins make these movements possible. The pilot uses levers and foot pedals to control the fins.

The octopus's funnel is positioned slightly below its eye.

containers attach to the boat. These containers take in water. Then, a cable around the containers squeezes the water out. This makes the boat move. The new system can be used on a variety of small watercraft. The containers are quieter than boat propellers. They are also safer. Fish cannot get caught in them.

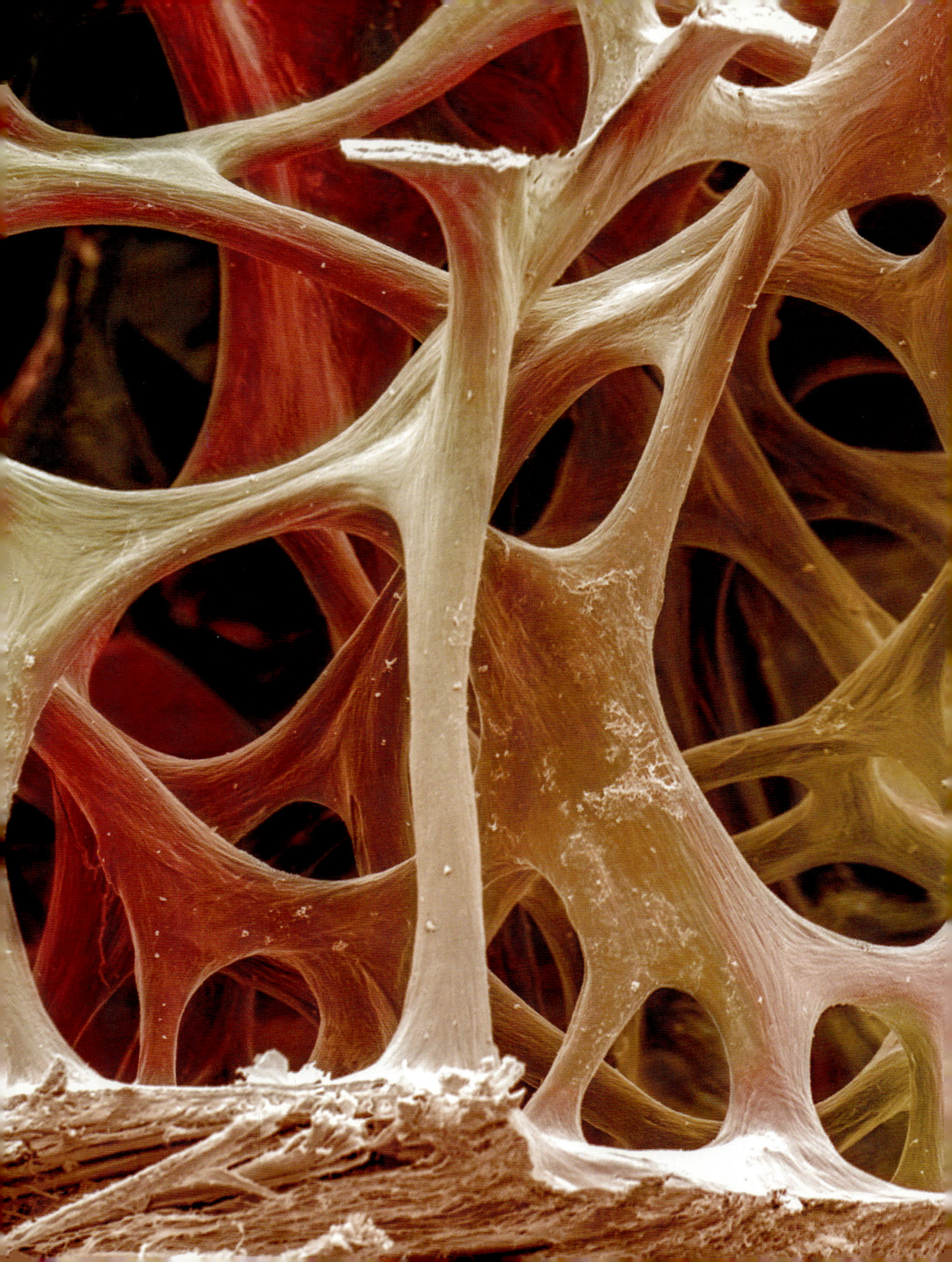

CHAPTER 4

IN THE FUTURE

Transportation technology is always changing. Nature has inspired many of today's transportation methods. Now, nature is paving the way for designs of the future.

One airplane company is designing a see-through plane. The plane's body is similar to the bone structure of birds.

Birds' bones are filled with pockets of air.

Bird bones are mostly hollow. Inside the bone, thin walls cross one another to make a web-like pattern. This makes the bones light but strong. The see-through plane will have a web of support beams. The beams provide strength only where necessary. This allows for more space between the beams. Large windows will fill the extra space. That way, people can see out and above the plane as they fly.

Nature is also inspiring future car designs. Engineers want to do a better job of preventing car crashes. They are studying how fish move. Fish swim in large groups called schools. However, they never run into one another. Each fish

Designers of the see-through plane hope to make it a reality by 2050.

adjusts its speed to match the speed of other fish.

Many new cars have a similar feature. The cars contain devices called sensors. The sensors measure the speeds of other cars. They can tell if other cars are nearby.

Driverless cars gather information about the cars around them.

The car uses this information to avoid crashing. It can speed up or slow down without direction from the driver. Some cars can automatically stop to avoid a crash.

Humans make many mistakes while driving. Driverless cars would use computers to remove error. These cars would have fish-like instincts. With fewer errors, humans could travel more safely.

A MOBILE ANT

In 2013, car designers took part in a design challenge. They designed cars using biomimicry. One group of designers came up with a car called the Mobilliant. The design is modeled after an ant. An ant takes in oxygen and other gases through its **exoskeleton**. The Mobilliant would take in gases through its lid. Then, it would turn the gases into **fertilizer**. The car would also have two tanks. This is similar to ants, which have two stomachs. The Mobilliant could even climb walls.

FOCUS ON

TRANSPORTATION TECHNOLOGY INSPIRED BY NATURE

Write your answers on a separate piece of paper.

1. Write a letter to a friend describing a technology featured in Chapter 3.

2. Which type of vehicle would you like to design after an animal? Why?

3. Which sea animal inspired the McLaren P1 car?

   A. sailfish
   B. octopus
   C. shark

4. What would happen if an airplane did not have winglets?

   A. The airplane would use more fuel.
   B. The airplane would fly faster and higher.
   C. The airplane would not be able to turn.

Answer key on page 32.

GLOSSARY

bacteria
Single-celled living things. They can be useful or harmful.

drag
The force of air pushing back against a moving object.

ducts
Tubes used to carry air.

efficient
Accomplishing as much as possible with as little effort or resources as possible.

exoskeleton
A skeleton outside the body. An exoskeleton supports and protects an animal's body.

fertilizer
A substance that helps plants grow.

fringe
A border of loose or hanging material in the shape of strips or strings.

lift
Upward movement.

parasites
Animals or plants that live on or in other living things.

TO LEARN MORE

BOOKS

Becker, Helaine. *Zoobots: Wild Robots Inspired by Real Animals*. Toronto: Kids Can Press, 2014.

Gifford, Clive. *Cars, Trains, Ships, and Planes*. New York: DK Publishing, 2015.

Yomtov, Nel. *From Termite Den to . . . Office Building*. Ann Arbor, MI: Cherry Lake Publishing, 2014.

NOTE TO EDUCATORS

Visit **www.focusreaders.com** to find lesson plans, activities, links, and other resources related to this title.

INDEX

Answer Key: 1. Answers will vary; **2.** Answers will vary; **3.** A; **4.** A